Debbie
the Duckling
Fairy

To Henry, who loves "quack quacks"

Special thanks to Rachel Elliot

Copyright © 2017 by Rainbow Magic Limited.

All rights reserved. Published by Scholastic Inc., *Publishers since 1920*. SCHOLASTIC and associated logos are trademarks and/or registered trademarks of Scholastic Inc. RAINBOW MAGIC is a trademark of Rainbow Magic Limited. Reg. U.S. Patent & Trademark Office and other countries. HIT and the HIT logo are trademarks of HIT Entertainment Limited.

The publisher does not have any control over and does not assume any responsibility for author or third-party websites or their content.

No part of this publication may be reproduced, stored in a retrieval system, or transmitted in any form or by any means, electronic, mechanical, photocopying, recording, or otherwise, without written permission of the publisher. For information regarding permission, write to Scholastic Inc., Attention: Permissions Department, 557 Broadway, New York, NY 10012.

ISBN 978-1-338-20689-0

10 9 8 7 6 5 4 3 2 1   18 19 20 21 22

Printed in the U.S.A.   40
First printing 2018

Debbie
the Duckling
Fairy

by Daisy Meadows

SCHOLASTIC INC.

The Fairyland
Palace

Farmhouse

Pond

Fluttering
Fairyland Farm

Greenfields Farm

Greenfields
House

Barn

Pond

I want a farm that's just for me,
With animals I won't set free.
It's far too slow to find each one.
Let fairy magic get this done!

With magic from the fairy farm,
I'll grant my wish—to their alarm!
And if I spoil the humans' fun,
Then Jack Frost really will have won!

Contents

A Merry Midterm

"It's so nice of your friends to invite me to the farm with you," said Rachel Walker.

Her best friend, Kirsty Tate, smiled. They were on their way to Greenfields Farm in the car with Mr. and Mrs. Tate. The farm was just outside Wetherbury, Kirsty's hometown, where the two best friends were spending their school break.

"Greenfields Farm is so cool," Kirsty said. "Mom and Dad have known the owners for years, and they were really happy to invite you to come along, too."

"Niall and Harriet Hawkins work very hard," said Mr. Tate. "They've been planning to open the farm to paying visitors for months."

"They were so pleased when we offered to help them set up for the opening at the end of this week," Mrs. Tate added.

"The new visitors are bound to love the little baby animals that were just born this spring," said Kirsty.

"I'm looking forward to seeing the babies the most," said Rachel. "I keep trying to decide which are my favorite baby animals, but I never can."

The car started to bump down the lane toward the farm. The girls rolled the back windows down, and a chorus of birdsong flooded into the car.

"That's better than any car radio," said Mrs. Tate. "What a beautiful sound."

"Look!" said Kirsty, pointing into the nearest field. "Look at all the animals. I can see cows . . . and sheep . . ."

"And there are some gorgeous horses over here," said Rachel, gazing out of the other window. "I wonder if we'll be allowed to ride them."

"I think we'll be too busy petting the sweet little foals," said Kirsty.

The girls shared an excited smile as the car stopped outside the farmhouse. It was made of reddish bricks, and the door and windows looked freshly painted. There were cheerful yellow curtains in every window.

A tall woman with straight blond hair strode around the side of the farmhouse and waved to them.

"That's Harriet," said Mrs. Tate, waving back.

"You're just in time," said Harriet, smiling as they all got out of the car.

"I'm sorry to put you to work right away, but we have an emergency. We have to mend a broken fence before one of the animals escapes or gets hurt on it."

"That's what we're here for," said Mr. Tate with a grin. "Lead the way, Harriet. We can unpack later."

"I'm so grateful that you're all here,"
said Harriet. "Come around to the barn
at the back of the farmhouse. Niall is just
finishing the milking."

The scent of honeysuckle filled the air
as Rachel and the Tates followed Harriet
around the side of the farmhouse. Outside
a small barn, a dark-haired
man was standing
beside a cow,
holding a
bucket
filled with
milk.

"Hello,
everyone,"
he said as
they walked
toward him.

"Welcome to the farm! Girls, this is Blossom. Would you like to say hello?"

Rachel and Kirsty felt very excited, but they made sure that they walked slowly, so they didn't startle Blossom. Soon they were patting and petting her, and she was gently mooing. The girls thought that she was the nicest cow they had ever seen, with her soft nose and her big, shining eyes.

"I can see that you two love animals,"

said Harriet. "Would you like to go and see the new ducklings at the pond while we mend the fence?"

"That would be awesome," said Kirsty.

"I'd love to!" said Rachel at exactly the same time.

Harriet pointed to a field on the right of the barn, while the girls danced up and down in excitement.

"That's where the broken fence is," she said. "If you need us, you'll find us there. The pond is down that path."

She pointed to where a path wound along the edge of a different field. It disappeared between two large trees.

"The pond is just past those trees," said Harriet. "Enjoy watching the ducklings, and come back when you're ready for a big Greenfields Farm dinner!"

Rachel and Kirsty hurried along the path. The row of bushes that marked the edge of the field was full of colorful wildflowers.

"Red campions, foxgloves, daisies . . . I can't decide which ones I like best," Kirsty said, running her hand along the top of the bushes as they walked.

"Let's pick some on our way back and put them in a jam jar in our room," Rachel said.

The girls held hands and walked through the trees that Harriet had pointed out. At once they saw a large pond sparkling in the sunshine, surrounded by tall cattails. Mother and father ducks lined the banks, resting in the sun while the tiny ducklings quacked and happily splashed in the water.

"Goodness, they are so loud," said Kirsty with a laugh. "I can't believe that something so small can make such a big noise."

But Rachel didn't reply, because she was gazing at the ducks' nest on the opposite bank of the pond.

"Look, Kirsty," she said in a low voice. "The nest is glowing."

The girls shared a thrilled smile, because they knew exactly what this meant. They were friends with the fairies, and they knew that the glow was magical. As they watched, the glow grew brighter, and then a tiny fairy flew out of the nest and swooped across the pond.

Creatures in the Clouds

"Hooray, I found you!" the little fairy cheered.

She looped over the noisy ducklings, who flapped their fluffy wings and quacked even more loudly. Her wings glimmered in the sunshine as she hovered in front of the girls.

"Hello," she said, smiling. "I'm Debbie the Duckling Fairy."

Debbie had wavy light-brown hair with blond tips and sparkling amber eyes. She was wearing a green T-shirt and a pair of blue shorts, and her gold necklace shone in the sunshine.

"I'm Rachel and this is Kirsty," said Rachel.

"Oh my, I know that!" said Debbie with a bubbly laugh. "I came here to find

you! A little bird told me that you were
here, and I came to look for you right
away. We've had some new arrivals at
the Fairyland Farm, too. Would you
like to come with me and see the baby
animals?"

"Oh yes, please!" said the girls together.

They knew that the grown-ups
wouldn't be worried. However long the
girls spent in Fairyland, not a single
moment would pass in the human world.
Debbie lifted her wand and flew around
the girls, trailing fairy dust behind her.
She went faster and faster, until she was
no more than a blur. Rachel and Kirsty
blinked and rubbed their eyes. When they
looked again, they were hovering with
pale, glittery fairy wings, high in the sky,
among big, fluffy white clouds.

"I'm so excited
that you're
here," said
Debbie,
who was
hovering
beside them.
"Welcome to the
Fluttering Fairyland Farm."

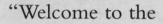

Rachel and Kirsty had to rub their
eyes again. In front of them, a large
green field was floating in midair. In the
far corner was a little cream-colored
farmhouse, with a red roof and green
shutters on the windows. Next to the
farmhouse, a round pond glimmered
in the sunshine. There was a barn with
a curved roof, and stalls with space for
three ponies inside.

But none of the buildings was as wonderful as the animals that lived in them. Tiny ducks glided across the pond, and little pink pigs snuffled in the trough. Goats sprang across a little brook, and the sheep looked like tiny white clouds on the grass.

A farmer was standing outside the farmhouse, watching over the animals and smiling.

"That's Francis, the Fairyland farmer," Debbie explained, waving to him. "And there are the other Farm Animal Fairies."

Three other fairies were playing with the farm animals. Debbie called to them, and they zoomed up from the magical farm at once.

"Welcome!" they said, gathering around their visitors and smiling. "We're so pleased you could come."

"I'd like you to meet Elodie the Lamb Fairy, Penelope the Foal Fairy, and Billie the Baby Goat Fairy," said Debbie.

"Together, we take care of the baby animals that are born each year, with the help of our magical baby animals."

"Come and meet Francis," said Elodie in a gentle voice.

Rachel and Kirsty flew down with the other fairies and landed beside Francis. He was wearing a yellow vest and a checked hat, and he smiled from ear to ear when he looked at Rachel and Kirsty.

"I'm very proud to welcome you here at last," he said. "I've heard a lot about you from the fairies."

"It looks like a really happy farm," said Rachel, gazing around. "You must really love all your animals."

Francis nodded. "We have lots of wonderful animals here," he said. "And I have lots of visits from Debbie, Elodie, Penelope, and Billie, because the magical baby farm animals live here, too."

"Oh, you must come and meet Splashy!" said Debbie, bouncing up and down and clapping her hands together. "He's my magical duckling, and he's so sweet and funny."

Splashy was playing with the

other ducklings in the pond. Even though he was the same size as them, Rachel and Kirsty could immediately tell which one he was. His fluffy feathers shone with a tint of gold, and there was something extra special about the look in his bright eyes.

"He's adorable," said Kirsty. "I'd love to meet all the animals you have here."

"And I'd love to introduce them to you," said Francis. "Follow me."

Kidnapped!

The fairies and Francis led Rachel and Kirsty to a daisy-filled meadow. A little white lamb came bouncing over to them.

"It's as if she has springs in her legs!" said Rachel, laughing at the sight. "And look, she has the same tint of gold in her wool as Splashy."

"This is Fluffy, my magical lamb," said Elodie.

"She's adorable," said Kirsty, stroking Fluffy's soft coat.

Next they met Frisky the foal. Penelope had to coax him out of his stall at first.

"He's a little shy," she said as Frisky snuggled into her arms.

"He's lovely," said Rachel in a kind voice.

Soon Frisky was nuzzling Rachel's arm,

and she felt as if she had made a new
friend.

"Come and meet Chompy," said Billie.

The magical baby
goat made everyone
laugh by trying to
push his nose into
Kirsty's pockets.

"He's very
curious," Billie said.

"I don't mind,"
said Kirsty with
a giggle.

Just then, Splashy
came flapping out of the pond to join
them, and everyone giggled as the
magical babies wobbled and waddled
around together on the bright-green
grass of the farm.

"There are plenty more animals to see," said Francis. "Come and meet the cows— there's a brand-new baby calf that I'm sure you'll love."

The fairies followed Francis toward the barn, leaving the magical babies playing. Inside, a little calf was standing beside his mother. He looked at the visitors and blinked his big, brown eyes.

"This is Toffee," said Francis in a soft

voice. "He's only one day old."

One by one, the fairies fluttered over to Toffee and stroked his brown coat. At first he was shy and pressed close against his mother, but after a little while he relaxed. Soon he was nuzzling the fairies and making happy, snuffly noises.

Suddenly, a rough cackle rang out across the farm. Toffee flinched at the sound and pressed against his mother again.

"I recognize that laugh," said Rachel in alarm.

Francis and the fairies zoomed out of the barn and came upon a horrible sight. Jack Frost and three goblins were standing on the grass in the middle of the farm. Jack Frost had Frisky tucked under his arm, and each of the other goblins had one of the magical animals, too. Jack Frost was smiling his most evil smile.

"Oh no!" cried Debbie.

"Stop, thieves!" Rachel called out.

Jack Frost cackled again.

"I don't take orders from silly little fairies," he said with an evil sneer.

"These animals do not belong to you," said Francis in a very stern voice. "Put them down at once."

Jack Frost stuck out his tongue and

replied with a long, loud raspberry.

"No way," he snapped. "My snow goose and her baby, Snowdrop, need some friends. So I'm going to make my very own petting zoo at my Ice Castle, starting with these animals."

"You can't just take these animals," Penelope exclaimed. "They're *our* friends, and this is their home."

Jack Frost ignored her and turned to his goblins.

"Meet me at the petting zoo," he ordered. "Here's some magic to get you there. I have to go and see my snow goose now."

He disappeared in a bolt of blue lightning, but the three goblins looked at one another with mischief on their faces.

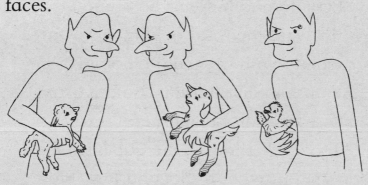

"They're glowing blue," said Rachel in astonishment.

"That's because Jack Frost has given them each a tiny bit of his magic," said Debbie.

"Goblins with their own magic?" said Elodie. "I don't like the sound of that."

"I want all the cuddles for myself," said the goblin holding Splashy.

"Me, too," said the one with Fluffy in his arms. "But how can we keep the animal babies away from Jack Frost?"

"Let's go and hide in the human world," said the third goblin, who was struggling with a wiggly Chompy.

"You shouldn't do that," said Kirsty. "Those animals belong here."

"Too late!" shouted the goblins. "You can't tell us what to do, and Jack Frost won't be able to find us when we hide away. We'll be the most famous goblins in Goblin Grotto."

They vanished in a flash of blue, taking the magical babies with them.

"We have to get back to the human world," said Debbie.

With a wave of Debbie's wand and a whoosh of fairy dust, the girls found themselves standing once again beside the pond at Greenfields Farm. Debbie was still with them, her eyes blazing.

"Poor Splashy will be so scared," she exclaimed. "That horrible Jack Frost—and those naughty goblins—how dare they steal our little friends away!"

"I'm sure Splashy knows that you will come and save him," said Rachel, trying to comfort the little fairy.

"It's not just Splashy I'm worried about," Debbie went on. "He helps me look after ducklings everywhere and keep them out of trouble. Without him, I don't know how to take care of them all."

Just then, the girls noticed that there was a lot of noise coming from the pond. All the grown-up ducks were swimming around in circles and quacking loudly.

"Are they looking for something?" asked Kirsty.

"I don't see a single duckling," Rachel exclaimed. "This pond was full of them last time we were here. Oh, Kirsty, where did all the ducklings go?"

Woof or Quack?

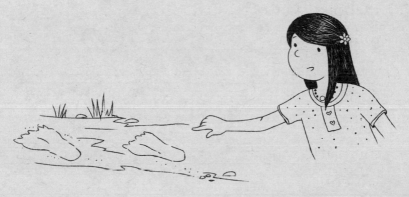

"It's happening already," said Debbie,
biting her lip. "Without Splashy by my
side, ducklings all over the human world
are going to get into trouble."

"Look over here," said Kirsty, peering
at the soft mud on the bank of the pond
and pointing. "Do these look like goblin
footprints to you?"

Large footprints were leading away
from the pond and along the path to the
farm. Rachel and Debbie nodded.

"Good eye," said
Debbie. "Let's
follow them."

"It'll be
easier to
follow
them if
we can
all fly," said
Rachel.

"Hide in the cattails, just in case
anyone comes along," said Debbie.

Rachel and Kirsty dove into the
cattails, and Debbie raised her wand.
Soon the three fairies were zooming over
Greenfields Farm, their eyes fixed on the

goblin footprints below. From high in the sky, the fields looked like a beautiful quilt.

"Look, there are Mom and Dad," said Kirsty, pointing down to the field where the grown-ups were mending the fence.

Nearby, Blossom was grazing in the pasture outside her barn. The goblin footprints led the fairies past Blossom and all the way to the farmhouse.

ar puppies yapping," said
peeding up. "Maybe something
set the farmhouse dogs."

"Something or some*one*," said Rachel.
"I'll bet it's someone green and grumpy.
The goblins probably scared the puppies."

"But Niall and Harriet don't have any
puppies," said Kirsty.

She and Rachel caught up with Debbie,
and they all landed in the yard. They were so
small that the gaps between the cobblestones
seemed as wide as country lanes.

"Let's hide around the side of the farmhouse and turn back into humans," said Rachel. "We'll have a better chance of stopping the goblins if we are big again."

The yapping from inside the farmhouse grew louder, and Debbie quickly transformed the girls into humans again. She darted into Rachel's pocket and the girls hurried into the farmhouse kitchen through the open door. They expected to see a basket full of playful puppies.

Instead, a crowd of fluffy little
ducklings surrounded them. They were
yapping, chasing their tails, and chewing
everything in sight. There wasn't a single
quack to be heard or waddle to be seen.

"Oh my goodness, the ducklings are
acting like puppies!" Kirsty exclaimed.

Rachel clutched Kirsty's arm and
pointed at a group of ducklings over by

the sink. One of them had feathers that
glimmered with a tint of gold.

"Debbie, I think we found Splashy!" she
said.

They heard a loud squawk,
and a goblin barreled across
the kitchen toward Splashy.

"Come here!" he
screeched. "I want to
cuddle you!"

The other
ducklings
scattered
sideways
as the

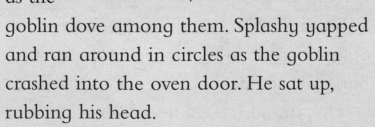

goblin dove among them. Splashy yapped
and ran around in circles as the goblin
crashed into the oven door. He sat up,
rubbing his head.

"I just want to cuddle," he wailed. "Splashy, don't run away from me. Come back!"

As he stood up and kept chasing Splashy, Debbie flew out of Rachel's pocket.

"These poor ducklings are so confused," she said, her voice shaking as she called out to the goblin. "Please go away! I need Splashy back so the ducklings can start acting like ducklings again."

The goblin paid no attention to her.

"Greenfields Farm can't open to visitors with ducklings that act like puppies," said Kirsty. "Please listen to us."

But the goblin continued to chase Splashy around the kitchen as the tiny barks of the ducklings grew even louder.

"He's too interested in Splashy to notice

us at the moment," said Rachel. "We have to get Splashy back before he does. But how?"

"I've got an idea," said Kirsty. "If the ducklings think they're puppies, then let's treat them as if they really are. Every puppy I've ever met has loved to chew slippers. Debbie, could you magic up a slipper for us?"

"Of course," said Debbie.

She flicked her wand, and a checked slipper appeared in Kirsty's hand. Kirsty waved it at Splashy.

"Come on, Splashy," she called. "Come and chew this lovely slipper!"

Goblin on the Cobbles

Splashy started running toward her, but then another duckling tugged the slipper out of Kirsty's hand. That duckling dashed into a corner and started chewing the slipper with his beak.

"We need another plan," said Rachel. "What else do puppies like? Walks . . .

games . . . I know! How about a game of fetch? Debbie, could you magic up a dog toy?"

In a flash, Rachel was holding a blue rubber toy in the shape of a duck. It quacked when she squeezed it, which made all the ducklings turn to look. Rachel squeezed it again and then threw it across the room.

"Fetch, Splashy," she called.

Splashy ran after the toy, yapping in excitement. But the goblin spotted him and lunged forward. This time, he managed to catch the little duckling in his long, bony fingers.

"Got you," he said. "Now you're mine!"

He raced out of the farmhouse kitchen into the cobblestone yard, clutching Splashy to his chest. Debbie zoomed after him.

"Come on," she called to Rachel and Kirsty. "We can't lose him this time."

The girls ran after the goblin, and all the other ducklings dashed after them. They scrambled between the girls' legs, making them stumble.

"They almost tripped us!" said Rachel.

"Oh, that gives me an idea," said Kirsty.

She raced back into the farmhouse and came out holding the blue rubber toy. She squeezed it and the ducklings turned to look.

"Fetch," said Kirsty.

She threw the toy across the yard, and it landed beside the goblin's big feet. Yapping, panting, and barking, the ducklings bounded after it. They bumped against and between the goblin's legs, knocking him this way and that. The goblin screeched, wobbled, and fell head over heels into a muddy puddle. In the confusion, he let go of Splashy.

At once, Rachel ran to scoop up the magical duckling. She held him gently in her arms and turned to Debbie.

"Splashy!" cried the Duckling Fairy in delight.

She flew to him with her arms held out wide. As soon as she touched him, he shrank to fairy size. Quacking, he snuggled up to Debbie.

"He's back to his old self," said Debbie, cuddling him and kissing his fluffy feathers.

"So are all the other ducklings," said Kirsty.

She smiled as the little ducklings waddled out of the yard toward the pond, quacking at the tops of their lungs.

"They're very noisy—whether they're being puppies *or* ducklings," said Rachel with a laugh.

The goblin was watching the ducklings waddle away, too, and he looked very sad. Kirsty felt sorry for him.

"Are you feeling worried about what Jack Frost will say?" she asked.

The goblin gave an awkward little wriggle as he looked at Kirsty.

"Yes, a bit," he said. "I expect there will be a lot of shouting when Jack Frost finds out that he won't have Splashy at his petting zoo. But most of all, I'm going to miss the sweet little ducklings. They're so soft and cuddly and cute."

"You can always visit a pond and see the ducklings splashing around," said Debbie. "Ducklings love visitors. But you have to promise that you will never again try to take one away. They belong with their moms and dads, just like Splashy belongs with me."

"I promise," said the goblin, cheering up at once. "I'm going to find a new duckling pond to visit right now."

After he ran off, Rachel, Kirsty, and Debbie exchanged happy smiles.

"We did it," said Rachel. "Splashy is safe, and the ducklings are back to normal before the grown-ups noticed anything was wrong."

"If we don't want the grown-ups to notice anything, we'd better clean up the farmhouse kitchen," said Kirsty, laughing. "Ducklings don't make neat and tidy houseguests!"

Rachel plucked a feather out of Kirsty's hair. "They sure don't!" she agreed.

The Mystery Cleaner

Laughing, they went back into the
farmhouse kitchen. It was covered in
feathers and the muddy prints of tiny
webbed feet. Bowls had been overturned,
cupboards and drawers had been emptied,
and dish towels had been chewed. The
contents of the kitchen pantry were spread
across the floor.

Kirsty and Rachel started to roll up their sleeves, but Debbie stopped them with a smile.

"Leave this to me," she said, raising her wand.

Splashy perched on Kirsty's fingertip, and they all watched as Debbie waved her wand and spoke the words of a spell.

"Sweep feathers up, wipe mud away.
Reverse what happened here today.
Return each item to its place,
And do not leave a single trace."

Instantly, the kitchen was spick-and-span.

Debbie fluttered over to the girls and took Splashy into her arms again.

"Thank you for helping me get him back," she said.

Splashy quacked loudly, and they all laughed.

"I think he's trying to say thank you, too," said Debbie with her bubbly laugh.

"It's good to see you so happy again," said Rachel. "We loved meeting you both—and being able to help."

"I can't wait to tell Francis and the other Farm Animal Fairies that Splashy is safe," Debbie went on. "I hope that we can find the other magical babies quickly, too."

"We'll do everything we can to help," Kirsty promised.

"I'm going to take Splashy back to the Fluttering Fairyland Farm now," said Debbie. "I hope I'll see you both again soon. Good-bye!"

As the girls waved, Debbie disappeared back to Fairyland in a flurry of sparkling fairy dust. At that moment, the girls heard footsteps on the cobblestones and voices laughing. Then Mr. and Mrs. Tate came in with Niall and Harriet.

"Here you are," said Mrs. Tate. "We

went to find you at the pond, but all we saw were the sweet little ducklings."

"They're very cute," said Rachel. "I think they're my favorite farm babies."

"I thought that lambs were your favorite farm babies," said Kirsty.

"All farm babies are my favorites," said Rachel with a laugh. "I can't choose between them!"

Niall and Harriet were gazing around the kitchen with wide eyes.

"What on earth's happened here?" asked Harriet.

The girls exchanged a worried look.

Had Debbie's magic missed something?

"We left the kitchen in a real mess this morning," said Niall. "Who cleaned it up for us? Girls, was it you?"

"It wasn't us," said Kirsty truthfully.

"You must have elves," said Mrs. Tate, laughing.

Harriet laughed, too.

"I'll take all the help I can get," she said. "There are only a few days until opening day, and we still have so much to do."

Soon everyone was sitting around the big farmhouse table, digging in to a delicious dinner.

"Why does working outside always make you so hungry?" asked Mr. Tate as he had his third helping.

Harriet looked at the girls.

"I'm glad you enjoyed meeting our ducklings," she said. "I hope that our visitors will love them, too."

"Of course they will," said Rachel. "The ducklings are so sweet and so much fun. I could watch them splashing around for hours."

"It's really interesting to see them play together while their moms and dads watch," Kirsty added. "They're just the same as little children at the park."

"You know, Harriet and I would really like some help with the baby animals over the next few days," Niall said. "Would you two like to be in charge of looking after them?"

"Really?" asked Kirsty, her eyes wide. "Oh yes, please."

"We'd love it," Rachel added.

"That's decided, then," said Harriet. "We'll show you what needs to be done in the morning."

As the grown-ups continued to chat, Rachel and Kirsty exchanged a secret glance. Looking after the baby animals sounded like the most delightful job on the farm.

"We've got three more animals to find before Greenfields Farm opens to visitors," Kirsty whispered to Rachel. "Looking after the animals here might help us to get the rest of the magical baby farm animals back from Jack Frost and the goblins."

"This is going to be an unforgettable spring break," said Rachel. "A whole week of magical adventures and sweet baby animals. I can't wait!"

RAINBOW magic

THE Farm Animal FAIRIES

Rachel and Kirsty found Debbie's
missing magic animal. Now it's
time for them to help

Elodie
the Lamb Fairy!

Join their next adventure in this
special sneak peek . . .

Alarm on the Farm

COCK-A-DOODLE-DOO!

Kirsty Tate and Rachel Walker sat up in bed at exactly the same moment. For a few seconds, they couldn't figure out where they were. Then they remembered and shared an excited smile.

"You know you're on a farm when a rooster is your alarm clock," said Rachel, bouncing out of bed. "Quick, let's get dressed. I can't wait to say good morning to all the animals."

This was their first full day at Greenfields Farm, just outside Wetherbury, where they were going to spend all of spring break. The farm was owned by Harriet and Niall Hawkins, friends of Kirsty's parents, and they were getting ready to open it up to paying visitors at the end of the week. The Tates and Rachel had come to help them.

Kirsty slipped out of bed, too, and threw open the yellow curtains. The walls of the farmhouse were so thick that the windowsill was big enough to sit on. Kirsty put the blanket from her bed on the sill, and then perched there, gazing out over the farm. She could see the barn where they had met Blossom the cow, and the trees that hid the sparkling duck pond. Over to the left, she could see a green pasture, with sheep dotted around it like little puffs of cotton wool.

"It's going to be a lovely sunny day," said Rachel, joining her at the window. "This is perfect weather for working outside."

"I wouldn't mind rain or snow, as long as we get to spend the day with baby animals," said Kirsty with a smile.

The day before, the Hawkinses had asked the girls to look after the baby animals on the farm. Rachel and Kirsty were thrilled. They both loved animals, and they usually found that animals loved them, too.

As soon as the girls were dressed and had made their beds, they hurried down the creaky farmhouse stairs to the big kitchen. Niall and Harriet Hawkins were already there with the Tates.

RAINBOW magic

Which Magical Fairies Have You Met?

- ❏ The Rainbow Fairies
- ❏ The Weather Fairies
- ❏ The Jewel Fairies
- ❏ The Pet Fairies
- ❏ The Sports Fairies
- ❏ The Ocean Fairies
- ❏ The Princess Fairies
- ❏ The Superstar Fairies
- ❏ The Fashion Fairies
- ❏ The Sugar & Spice Fairies
- ❏ The Earth Fairies
- ❏ The Magical Crafts Fairies
- ❏ The Baby Animal Rescue Fairies
- ❏ The Fairy Tale Fairies
- ❏ The School Day Fairies
- ❏ The Storybook Fairies
- ❏ The Friendship Fairies

SCHOLASTIC

HIT entertainment

Find all of your favorite fairy friends at
scholastic.com/rainbowmagic

RMFAIRY17

SPECIAL EDITION

Which Magical Fairies Have You Met?

- ❑ Joy the Summer Vacation Fairy
- ❑ Holly the Christmas Fairy
- ❑ Kylie the Carnival Fairy
- ❑ Stella the Star Fairy
- ❑ Shannon the Ocean Fairy
- ❑ Trixie the Halloween Fairy
- ❑ Gabriella the Snow Kingdom Fairy
- ❑ Juliet the Valentine Fairy
- ❑ Mia the Bridesmaid Fairy
- ❑ Flora the Dress-Up Fairy
- ❑ Paige the Christmas Play Fairy
- ❑ Emma the Easter Fairy
- ❑ Cara the Camp Fairy
- ❑ Destiny the Rock Star Fairy
- ❑ Belle the Birthday Fairy
- ❑ Olympia the Games Fairy
- ❑ Selena the Sleepover Fairy

- ❑ Cheryl the Christmas Tree Fairy
- ❑ Florence the Friendship Fairy
- ❑ Lindsay the Luck Fairy
- ❑ Brianna the Tooth Fairy
- ❑ Autumn the Falling Leaves Fairy
- ❑ Keira the Movie Star Fairy
- ❑ Addison the April Fool's Day Fairy
- ❑ Bailey the Babysitter Fairy
- ❑ Natalie the Christmas Stocking Fairy
- ❑ Lila and Myla the Twins Fairies
- ❑ Chelsea the Congratulations Fairy
- ❑ Carly the School Fairy
- ❑ Angelica the Angel Fairy
- ❑ Blossom the Flower Girl Fairy
- ❑ Skyler the Fireworks Fairy
- ❑ Giselle the Christmas Ballet Fairy
- ❑ Alicia the Snow Queen Fairy

▌SCHOLASTIC

Find all of your favorite fairy friends at
scholastic.com/rainbowmagic

3 stories in each one!

HIT entertainment

RMSPECIAL20